MAGIC MASTERS

Dalmatian Press, LLC, 2006. All Rights Reserved. Printed in the U.S.A.
The DALMATIAN PRESS name and logo are trademarks of Dalmatian Press, LLC, Franklin, Tennessee 37067.
No part of this book may be reproduced or copied in any form without written permission of Dalmatian Press,
BVS Entertainment, Inc., and BVS International N.V.

15571 Power Rangers Mystic Force: Magic Masters

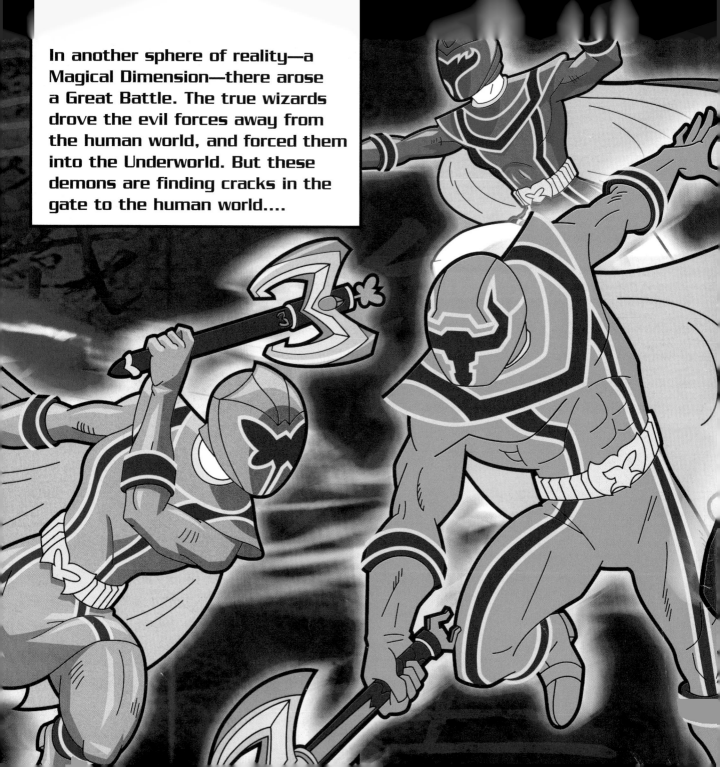

In another sphere of reality—a Magical Dimension—there arose a Great Battle. The true wizards drove the evil forces away from the human world, and forced them into the Underworld. But these demons are finding cracks in the gate to the human world....

Udonna, the sorceress, has chosen five brave teens to fight the evil demons. These mystical warriors are the Mystic Force Power Rangers!

Xander is the Green Mystic Ranger, of great agility and strength. The elements of earth become his weapons.

Vida is the Pink Mystic Ranger, sister to Madison. She is a shape-shifter with the power of wind and air.

Chip is the Yellow Mystic Ranger, who can control light and electricity.

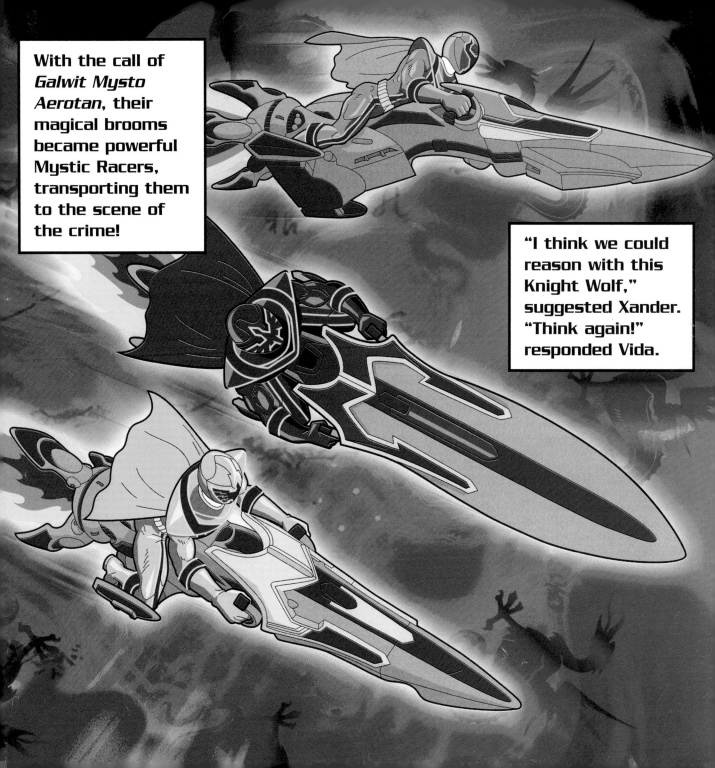

With the call of *Galwit Mysto Aerotan*, their magical brooms became powerful Mystic Racers, transporting them to the scene of the crime!

"I think we could reason with this Knight Wolf," suggested Xander. "Think again!" responded Vida.

With the powers of nature, the five Mystic Rangers battled and destroyed the Hidiacs!

"How'd you like *that* heat, Koragg?" taunted Nick.

"You have not yet felt the power of the dark magic!" replied Koragg. "*Uthe Mejor!*"

Koragg's spell transformed him into a giant warrior— towering over the Rangers.

"Whoa!" said Vida. "That leaves me feeling a bit winded!"

Faced with the power of the Mystic Titans, Koragg called forth his Horse Zord—Catastros.

"*Uthe Mejor Catastros!* Ride up from your depths!"

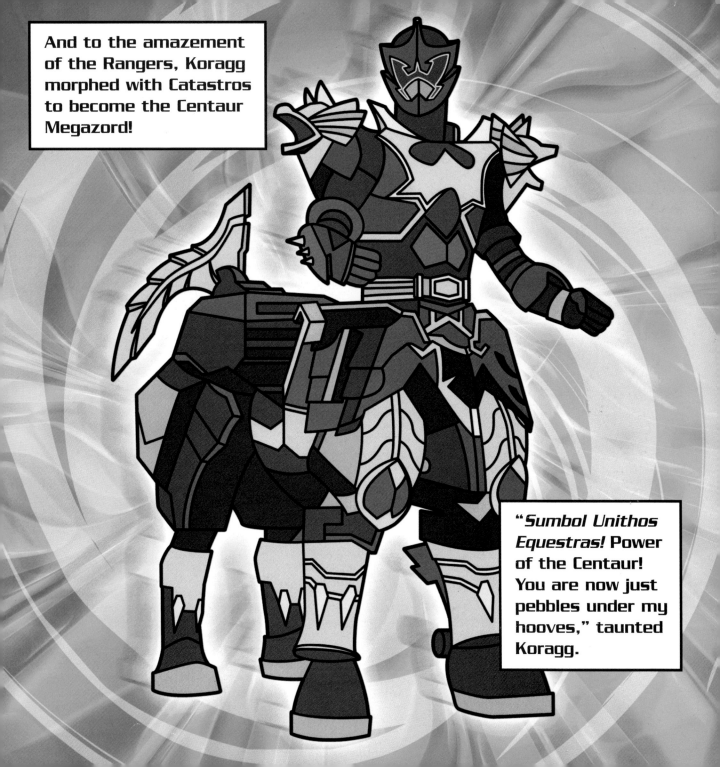

And to the amazement of the Rangers, Koragg morphed with Catastros to become the Centaur Megazord!

"*Sumbol Unithos Equestras!* Power of the Centaur! You are now just pebbles under my hooves," taunted Koragg.

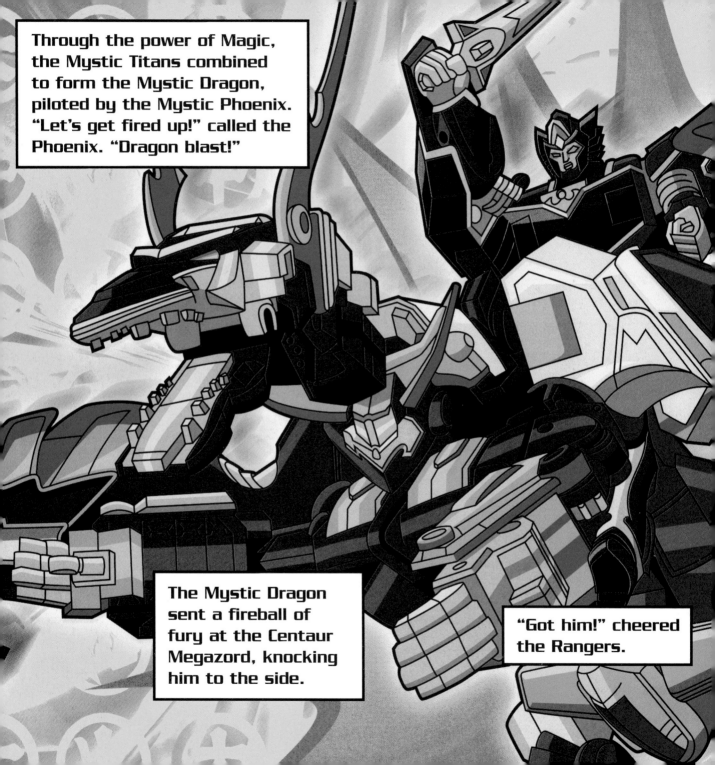

Through the power of Magic, the Mystic Titans combined to form the Mystic Dragon, piloted by the Mystic Phoenix. "Let's get fired up!" called the Phoenix. "Dragon blast!"

The Mystic Dragon sent a fireball of fury at the Centaur Megazord, knocking him to the side.

"Got him!" cheered the Rangers.

"You cheer too fast, Rangers," said Koragg as he raised his great shield. "Wolf attack! Behold the Eye of the Master!"

The great shield opened to reveal an eye—powerful and deadly—that shot a laser of intense force at the Mystic Dragon, knocking it to the ground. "Ha, ha, Rangers! *Now* it is *I* who cheer!"

"Checkmate! He's done for!" yelled Nick.

The defeated Koragg glared at the Rangers. "This was just one battle. Next time the outcome will be different!"

And with a call of "*Uthe Sastos!*" Koragg transported himself to the depths of the Underworld.

"Right! And next time, I'm going to reason with him!" announced Xander.
Vida gave him a sideways glance. "Ya think?"

Memories of a Lifetime™

Animals

ARTWORK FOR SCRAPBOOKS AND FABRIC-TRANSFER CRAFTS

Kathy Alpert

Sterling Publishing Co., Inc. New York
A Sterling/Chapelle Book

Author: Kathy Alpert

Kathy Alpert has been captivated by vintage postcards since she discovered them in the barn at her grandfather's New Hampshire farmhouse. She has since combed flea markets, antique shops, and attics around the country, accumulating more than 15,000 postcards from "The Golden Age." In 2001, she gave up her PR business and launched, PostMark Press, a greeting card line based on whimsical postcard images. Now a recognized authority on the subject, she has appeared on national television and in magazines. From her New England base, Kathy writes, designs, and works with manufacturers to create products using her postcards. She is excited to share part of her collection with other crafters.
E-mail Kathy at ksa@postmarkpress.com.
Visit Kathy on the Web at www.postmarkpress.com.

Book Designer: Karla Haberstich

If you have any questions or comments, please contact:
Chapelle, Ltd.
P.O. Box 9252, Ogden, UT 84409
(801) 621-2777 • (801) 621-2788 Fax
e-mail: chapelle@chapelleltd.com
Web site: www.chapelleltd.com

Memories of a Lifetime is a trademark of Sterling Publishing Co., Inc.

PC Configuration: Windows 98 or later with 128 MB RAM or greater. At least 100 MB of free hard disk space. Dual speed or faster CD-ROM drive, and a 24-bit color monitor.

Macintosh Configuration: Mac OS 9 or later with 128 MB RAM or greater. At least 100 MB of free hard disk space. Dual speed or faster CD-ROM drive, and a 24-bit color monitor.

10 9 8 7 6 5 4 3 2 1

Published by Sterling Publishing Co., Inc.
387 Park Avenue South, New York, NY 10016
© 2006 by Sterling Publishing Co., Inc.
Distributed in Canada by Sterling Publishing
c/o Canadian Manda Group, 165 Dufferin Street
Toronto, Ontario, Canada M6K 3H6
Distributed in the United Kingdom by GMC Distribution Services,
Castle Place, 166 High Street, Lewes, East Sussex, England BN7 1XU
Distributed in Australia by Capricorn Link (Australia) Pty. Ltd.
P. O. Box 704, Windsor, NSW 2756, Australia
Printed and Bound in China
All Rights Reserved

Sterling ISBN 1-4027-2879-4

For information about custom editions, special sales, premium and corporate purchases, please contact Sterling Special Sales Department at 800-805-5489 or specialsales@sterlingpub.com.

InTroducTion

Imagine having hundreds of rare vintage images right at your fingertips. With our *Memories of a Lifetime*™ series, that's exactly what you get. We've scoured antique stores, estate sales, and other outlets to find one-of-a-kind images to give your projects the flair that only old-time artwork can provide. From Victorian postcards to hand-painted beautiful borders and frames, it would take years to acquire a collection like this. However, with this easy-to-use resource, you'll have them all—right here, right now.

Each image has been reproduced to the highest quality standard for photocopying and scanning; reduce or enlarge them to suit your needs. A CD-Rom containing all of the images in digital form is included, enabling you to use them for any computer project over and again. If you prefer to use them as they're printed, simply cut them out—they're printed on one side only.

Perfect for paper crafting, scrapbooking, and fabric transfers, *Memories of a Lifetime* books will inspire you to explore new avenues of creativity. We've included a sampling of ideas to get you started, but the best part is using your imagination to create your own fabulous projects. Be sure to look for other books in this series as we continue to search the markets for wonderful vintage images.

How to Use This Book

General Instructions:

These images are printed on one side only, making it easy to simply cut out the desired image. However, you'll probably want to use them again, so we have included a CD-Rom which contains all of the images individually as well as in the page layout form. The CDs can be used with both PC and Mac formats. Just pop in the disk. On a PC, the file will immediately open to the Home page, which will walk you through how to view and print the images. For Macintosh® users, you will simply double-click on the icon to open. The images may also be incorporated into your computer projects using simple imaging software that you can purchase specifically for this purpose—a perfect choice for digital scrapbooking.

The reference numbers printed on the back of each image in the book are the same ones used on the CD, which will allow you to easily find the image you are looking for. The numbering consists of the book abbreviation, the page number, the image number, and the file format. The first file number (located next to the page number) is for the entire page. For example, AN01-001.jpg would be the entire image for page 1 of *Animals*. These are provided for you on the CD. The second file number is for the top-right image. The numbers continue in a counterclockwise spiral fashion.

Once you have resized your images, added text, created a scrapbook page, etc., you are ready to print them out. Printing on cream or white cardstock, particularly a textured variety, creates a more authentic look. You won't be able to tell that it's a reproduction! If you don't have access to a computer or printer, that's ok. Most photocopy centers can resize and print your images for a nominal fee, or they have do-it-yourself machines that are easy to use.

Ideas for Using the Images:

Scrapbooking:
These images are perfect for both heritage and modern scrapbook pages. Simply use the image as a frame, accent piece, or border. For those of you with limited time, the page layouts in this book have been created so that you can use them as they are. Simply print out or photocopy the desired page, attach a photograph into one of the boxes, and you have a beautiful scrapbook page in minutes. For a little dimension, add a ribbon or charm. Be sure to print your images onto acid-free cardstock so the pages will last a lifetime.

Cards:
Some computer programs allow images to be inserted into a card template, simplifying cardmaking. If this is not an option, simply use the images as accent pieces on the front or inside of the card. Use a bone folder to score the card's fold to create a more professional look.

Decoupage/Collage Projects:
For decoupage or collage projects, photocopy or print the image onto a thinner paper such as copier paper. Thin paper adheres to projects more effectively. Decoupage medium glues and seals the project, creating a gloss or matte finish when dry, thus protecting the image. Vintage images are beautiful when decoupaged to cigar boxes, glass plates, and even wooden plaques. The possibilities are endless.

Fabric Arts:
Vintage images can be used in just about any fabric craft imaginable: wall hangings, quilts, bags, or baby bibs. Either transfer the image onto the fabric by using a special iron-on paper, or by printing the image directly onto the fabric, using a temporary iron-on stabilizer that stabilizes the fabric to feed through a printer. These items are available at most craft and sewing stores. If the item will be washed, it is better to print directly on the fabric. For either method, follow the instructions on the package.

Wood Transfers:
It is now possible to "print" images on wood. Use this exciting technique to create vintage plaques, clocks, frames, and more. A simple, inexpensive transfer tool is available at most large craft or home improvement stores, or online from various manufacturers. You simply place the photocopy of the image you want, face down, onto the surface and use the tool to transfer the image onto the wood. This process requires a copy from a laser printer, which means you will probably have to get your copies made at a copy center. Refer to manufacturer's instructions for additional details. There are other transfer products available that can be used with wood. Choose the one that is easiest for you.

Gallery of Ideas

These *Animals* images can be used in a variety of projects: cards, scrapbook pages, and decoupage projects to name a few. The images can be used as they are shown in the layout, or you can copy and clip out individual images, or even portions or multitudes of images. The following pages contain a collection of ideas to inspire you to use your imagination and create one-of-a-kind treasures.

Many of the designs in this book invite you to replace portions of the original image with personalized photographs, sentiments, and journaling. This example retains the original quote and frame while replacing the dog images with photos of Buster.

BUSTER

DREAMS

BIG

Dogs are not our whole life, but they make our lives whole. —Roger Caras

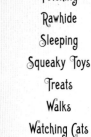

Doggy Dreams Page

Buster's Favorites:

Fetching
Rawhide
Sleeping
Squeaky Toys
Treats
Walks
Watching Cats

If only cats grew into kittens. —Robert A. M. Stern

*John
&
Scooter*

The "John & Scooter" photo was trimmed to cover two kitten drawings on the original page. Customized layouts such as this are easy to achieve with the versatile images in *Memories of a Lifetime: Animals.*

A wide selection of images enables you to honor all of your pets with pages of their own.

Sweet Kitty Page

To preserve the vintage look of the original image, black-and-white photographs were used.

He'll Give You
His Heart Page

original page

Give A HORSE WHAT *he* NEEDS AND HE *will* GIVE YOU HIS HEART IN *return.*

—Anonymous

CARTE POSTALE

Tous les pays étrangers n'acceptent pas la Correspondance au recto
Se renseigner à la poste

CORRESPONDANCE   ADRESSE

I'm having a great time with Grandpa. I feed the horses every day.

To:
Mom & Dad

The open space on a postcard is the perfect place for a personal message or journaling.

A classic image of a girl dressed for riding with the hounds graces unglazed ceramic squares to form these coasters. For this project, use a transfer paper that is designed for photocopiers and follow the manufacturer's instructions. A hard-drying paper adhesive provides a protective matte finish.

Charming Coasters

On the Farm Jigsaw Puzzle

Creating a one-of-a-kind puzzle is easy with *Memories of a Lifetime*. Mount the desired image to a premade jigsaw puzzle and cut the shapes free with a craft knife. Seal the edges of the individual pieces for longer-lasting fun.

Easter
Greetings Bag

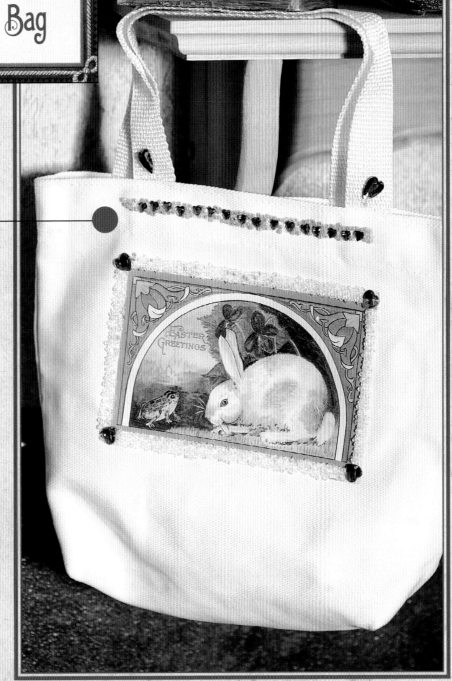

Applying images to
fabric is easy. To create
this Easter bag, print
the image of a rabbit
onto T-shirt transfer
paper and follow
the manufacturer's
instructions to apply it
to your bag. Finish by
gluing miniature beads
and embellishments
around the border.

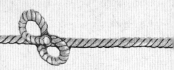

Enhance a book with a pretty playful bookmark. To create this look, mount and seal an image of a kitty couple on gold cardstock. Punch a hole and add a gold tassel to finish.

Cat Wedding Bookmark

Jeweled Travel Tins

Dogs are not our whole life,
but they make our lives whole.

—Roger Caras

Transform a common tin into a treasure by painting and sealing its surfaces, then gluing images onto the top and bottom. Apply a second layer of sealer; when dry, embellish with jewels.

Adding insets, such as a quote and the image of a child embracing a beloved dog, makes each tin a pleasure to open.

A lightweight wooden container becomes a trinket box when decoupaged with an animal choir. Prepare the canister, with a coat of acrylic paint, then apply the image with sealer and use glue to embellish with jewels. If the canister is large, simply copy the selected image and wrap one copy around each side.

Dressing Table Canister

Standard Arts
POST CARD

Correspondence

Address

Dogs are miracles with paws.

—Attributed to
Susan Ariel Rainbow Kennedy

AN01-003   AN01-002

                                            AN01-008

AN01-004   AN01-007

AN01-005   AN01-006

01 — AN01-001

Dogs are not our whole life, but they make our lives whole. —Roger Caras

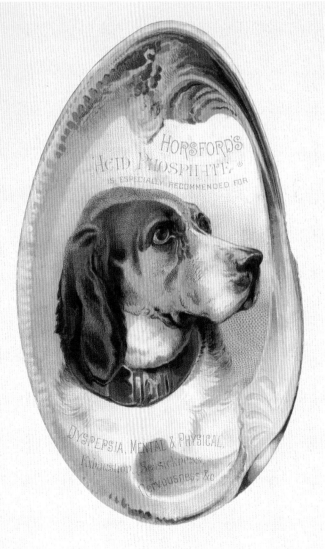

AN02-003

AN02-002

AN02-004

AN02-005

AN02-006

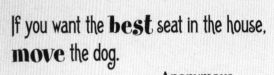

If you want the **best** seat in the house, **move** the dog.

—Anonymous

AN03-003   AN03-002

AN03-004

AN03-005   AN03-008

AN03-006   AN03-007

Still waitin' !

I got your note !

"Why Can't We Always Be Together ?"

"My love, a love that's through and through. For my loyal friend, my dog, that's you."

— Anonymous

A Short Tale with a Sad Ending.

AN04-004   AN04-003   AN04-002

AN04-005   AN04-009   AN04-008

AN04-006   AN04-007

Some days you're the dog;
some days you're the hydrant**.**

Love me, Love my dog.

AN05-003

AN05-002

AN05-004

AN05-008

AN05-005

AN05-007

AN05-006

05 — AN05-001

Bones is bones; but I'd
sooner have a letter, see?

I ain't one of those
college mutts, see?

AN06-004　　　　　　　　　　　AN06-003　　　　AN06-002

AN06-008

AN06-005

AN06-006

AN06-001　　　　　　　　　　　　　　　AN06-007

COCKER SPANIELS

The perils of duck **hunting** are great—especially for the **duck**.

—**Walter Cronkite**

AN07-003   AN07-002

AN07-004   AN07-007

AN07-005   AN07-006

07 — AN07-001

A SOCIAL PARTY

Now they'll blame me for this?

AN08-003

AN08-002

AN08-004

AN08-007

AN08-005

AN08-006

AN08-001

Dogs wait for us faithfully.
—Marcus Tullius Cicero

"Japs Pride"

FOXHOUNDS

AN09-003   AN09-002

AN09-004

AN09-005   AN09-008

AN09-006   AN09-007

TUCK'S POST CARD.

CARTE POSTALE. —————— POSTKARTE.

IF SENT ABROAD, THIS SPACE MAY ONLY BE USED
FOR NAME AND ADDRESS OF SENDER.

(FOR ADDRESS ONLY)

Best Wishes.

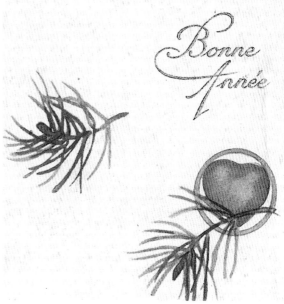

Bonne Année

AN10-003   AN10-002

                                  AN10-006

AN10-004   AN10-005

A HAPPY CHRISTMAS

Christmas Greetings!

Christmas Greetings

The Seasons
Greetings
To You

AN11-003   AN11-002

                                       AN11-006

AN11-004   AN11-005

11 — AN11-001

A Merry
Christmas.

To Wish you a merry Christmas

Christmas Greetings

Christmas

May
You have
A
Merry
Christmas

AN12-003   AN12-002

AN12-004   AN12-007

AN12-005   AN12-006

AN12-001

It is impossible to keep a straight face in the presence of one or more kittens.

—Cynthia E. Varnado

We are very lively
As you can see
Which makes us
as graceful
As we can be.

Clivette.

THE ASTRONOMERS.

MY MASTER'S HAT.

AN13-004   AN13-003   AN13-002

AN13-005   AN13-009

AN13-006

AN13-007   AN13-008

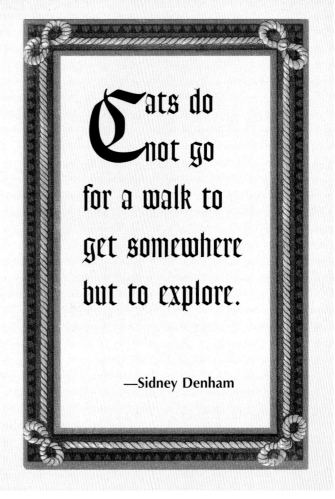

Cats do
not go
for a walk to
get somewhere
but to explore.

—Sidney Denham

BREAKING THE NEWS.

AN14-003

AN14-002

AN14-004

AN14-007

AN14-005

AN14-006

AN14-001

If only cats grew into kittens. ——Robert A. M. Stern

AN15-003

AN15-002

AN15-004

AN15-005

AN15-009

AN15-006

AN15-008

AN15-007

AN15-001

OUT FOR AN AIRING

Like a
graceful vase,
a cat, even when
motionless,
seems to *flow*.

—George F. Will

AN16-003   AN16-002

AN16-004   AN16-007

AN16-005   AN16-006

"STRICTLY IN IT."

ONE POUND CHESTS.

HALF POUND CHESTS.

JUNGLE CHOP FORMOSA TEA.

BIRTHDAY GREETINGS

AN17-003

AN17-002

AN17-004

AN17-007

AN17-005

AN17-006

May
a nice
little witch
brew a
Happy Hallowe'en
for you

Black cat
or white cat:
If it can catch
mice, it's a
good cat.

—Chinese Proverb

May fortune
smile on you.

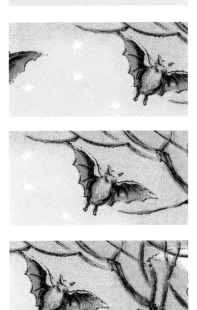

HALLOWE'EN GREETING

A bat and a cat, green-
eyed pumpkins, too.
A nice crawly mouse and
best wishes for YOU

AN18-003

AN18-002

AN18-011

AN18-004

AN18-010

AN18-009

AN18-008

AN18-005

AN18-007

AN18-006

18 — AN18-001

THANKSGIVING GREETINGS

THANKSGIVING JOYS

THANKSGIVING GREETINGS

Thanksgiving Greetings

AN19-004

AN19-003

AN19-002

AN19-007

AN19-005

AN19-006

19 ─ AN19-001

Thanksgiving Greetings

Hearty Thanksgiving Greetings.

Thanksgiving Joys

A JOLLY THANKSGIVING

Thanksgiving, to be truly **Thanksgiving**, is first thanks, then giving.

—Anonymous

Hearty Thanksgiving Greetings.

AN20-003   AN20-002

AN20-004   AN20-008

AN20-005

AN20-006   AN20-007

Thanksgiving Day

Greeting Thanksgiving.

THANKSGIVING

May glad Thanksgivings

Crown your days and years.

CORDIAL GREETINGS

Thanksgiving Greetings

POST CARD

4116

Novelty Mfg. & Art Co. Ltd., Montreal

Generous
and kindly acts
Should never once
be thought a tax
For generous
and kindly axe
Prepares your turkey:
these are facts.

GRAND DINNER
IN HONOR OF

Thanksgiving

Soup

THE LAST
THURSDAY
IN NOVEMBER

CHICKEN SOUP

WELL WATER

ROAST TURKEY
CRANBERRY
SAUCE

Vegetables

POTATOES.

CARROTS

PEAS

CIDER

Dessert

COFFEE

RAISINS

NUTS

Toast
May the turkey look thinner
At the end of this dinner

Thanksgiving Day Greetings.

AN21-004

AN21-003

AN21-002

AN21-005

AN21-009

AN21-006

AN21-007

AN21-008

There is one day that is ours. Thanksgiving Day . . . is the one day that is purely American.

—O. Henry

THE DAY WE HAVE TWO NATIONAL BIRDS

"May one give us peace in all our states,
The other a piece for all our plates."

AN22-004   AN22-003   AN22-002

AN22-005   AN22-008

AN22-006   AN22-007

AN22-001

If I hadn't started painting,
I would have raised chickens.

—Grandma Moses

AN23-003   AN23-002

AN23-004

AN23-005   AN23-008

AN23-006   AN23-007

AN23-001

Ein frohes OSTERFEST

Cheep Cheep!

BEST
Wishes for Easter

BEST EASTER WISHES

AN24-003   AN24-002

AN24-004   AN24-007

AN24-005   AN24-006

AN24-001

Easter Greetings

Христосъ Воскресе

If you were born lucky, even your **ROOSTER** will lay eggs.

—Russian Proverb

EASTER GREETINGS

EASTER GREETINGS

Where the **rooster** crows there is a village.

—Schambala Proverb

AN25-003   AN25-002

                                  AN25-008

AN25-004   AN25-007

AN25-005   AN25-006

Easter Greetings

DRESSED FOR DINNER

"Said The
big Black Rooster
To the
little Black Hen,
You haven't laid
An Egg in
'God knows When'
Said The
little Black Hen
To the
big Black Rooster,
You don't come
round as Often as
You useter."

Fröhliche Ostern

Best Easter Wishes

AN26-004   AN26-003   AN26-002

AN26-005   AN26-007

AN26-006

EASTER GREETING

A Joyous Eastertide

Life may not be the party we hoped for,
but while we're here we should dance.

—Anonymous

A very Happy EASTER to you.

A Bright and Happy Easter

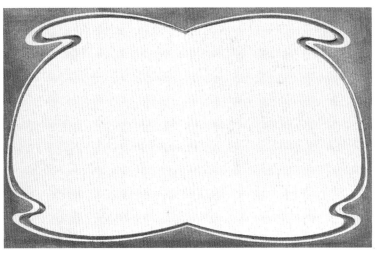

AN27-003   AN27-002

AN27-004

AN27-005

AN27-006   AN27-007

AN27-001

*Spring
hath
put a
spirit of
youth in
everything.*

—William
Shakespeare

A HAPPY
EASTERTIDE

AN28-004　　　　　　　　　　　　　AN28-003　　　　　　AN28-002

AN28-005

AN28-006　　　　　　　　　　　　　　　　AN28-007

Best
Easter Wishes

Best
EASTER
Wishes

To Wish you
A HAPPY
EASTER

A Joyous
Easter

Faith is putting all your eggs in God's basket, then counting your blessings before they hatch.

—Ramona C. Carroll

AN29-002

AN29-003   AN29-008

AN29-004

AN29-005   AN29-006   AN29-007

AN29-001

Easter Greetings

Easter Greeting

To Wish you
A Happy
Easter

People who count their chickens before
they are hatched, act very wisely, because
chickens run about so absurdly that it is
impossible to count them accurately.

—Oscar Wilde

Happy be
your
Easter

AN30-003   AN30-002

AN30-004   AN30-008

AN30-005

AN30-006   AN30-007

Don't put all your **eggs** in one basket.

—Unknown

AN31-003   AN31-002

AN31-004   AN31-008

AN31-005   AN31-007

AN31-006

Good Wishes for Easter

I think of the garden after the rain; And hope to my heart comes singing, At morn the cherry~blooms will be white, And the Easter bells be ringing!

—Edna Dean Procter, Easter Bells

POST CARD

MADE IN U.S.A.

FOR CORRESPONDENCE   FOR ADDRESS ONLY

EASTER GREETING

EASTER Greetings

Easter Greeting

AN34-003

AN34-002

AN34-004

AN34-005

AN34-008

AN34-006

AN34-007

AN34-001

POST CARD

Nun haben wir Beide das Körbchen voll
Und setzen uns fröhlich nieder,
Und singen: „Wie ist das Osterfest schön,
O, käme doch balde es wieder!"

Fröhliche
Ostern

Happy Easter Tide

Now
I know what
Love is.

—Virgil

AN35-003

AN35-002

AN35-004

AN35-007

AN35-005

AN35-006

AN35-001

PEACEFUL EASTER TIDE

Merry Easter!

I think there's a little child in all of us and we all too often forget to let the child out to play.

—Donna A. Favors

Easter Greeting

Just a wish for joy and gladness to be with you and yours all this Easter Day

WITH LOVING WISHES FOR A HAPPY EASTER.

Loving Easter Greetings

A Joyful Easter

AN36-004   AN36-003   AN36-002

AN36-005   AN36-009

AN36-006   AN36-007   AN36-008

Ideas are like **rabbits**. You get a couple and learn how to handle them, and pretty soon you have a dozen.

—John Steinbeck

AN37-003   AN37-002

AN37-004

AN37-005   AN37-008

AN37-006   AN37-007

AN37-001

BEST WISHES FOR EASTER

Easter Greeting

Easter Greeting

A Loving Easter

BEST EASTER WISHES

Love & eggs
are best when they are fresh.

—Russian Proverb

AN38-003   AN38-002

AN38-004   AN38-008

AN38-005

AN38-006   AN38-007

AN38-001

Merry Easter.

Without a shepherd, sheep are not a flock.

—Russian Proverb

A HAPPY EASTER.

A happy Easter

AN39-004   AN39-003   AN39-002

AN39-005   AN39-008

AN39-006   AN39-007

Brockton Fair

A *Horse!* A *Horse!*

My kingdom for a horse!

—Shakespeare

AN40-004   AN40-003   AN40-002

AN40-005   AN40-009

AN40-006   AN40-007   AN40-008

Riding: The art of keeping a horse between YOU and the ground.

—Author Unknown

AN41-003   AN41-002

AN41-004   AN41-008

AN41-005

AN41-006   AN41-007

Give A HORSE WHAT *he* NEEDS AND HE *will* GIVE YOU HIS HEART IN *return.*

—Anonymous

CARTE POSTALE

Tous les pays étrangers n'acceptent pas la Correspondance au recto

Se renseigner à la poste

CORRESPONDANCE   ADRESSE

AN42-003   AN42-002

AN42-004   AN42-007

AN42-005   AN42-006

AN42-001

In riding a **HORSE,** we borrow **FREEDOM.**

—Helen Thomson

No hour of *life* **is WASTED THAT IS SPENT** *in* the saddle.

—Winston Churchill

AN43-003

AN43-002

AN43-004

AN43-007

AN43-005

AN43-006

AN43-001

CHRISTMAS
GREETINGS.

With best
Christmas Wishes

·A·Merry·Christmas·

With peaceful joys your
home be bright.
Though skies be chill and grey.
May all your heart desires unite
To bless your Christmas Day

AN44-003   AN44-002

AN44-004

AN44-005   AN44-006

STICK TO YOUR SADDLE

YOU CAN TELL A TRUE **COWBOY** BY THE TYPE OF HORSE THAT HE RIDES.

—Cowboy Proverb

A **COWBOY** is a man with guts and a horse.

—William James

AN45-003   AN45-002

AN45-004   AN45-007

AN45-005   AN45-006

45 — AN45-001

HOLY COW!
—Harry Caray

AN46-003

AN46-002

AN46-004

AN46-008

AN46-005

AN46-006

AN46-007

46 — AN46-001

Trouble with
a Milk cow
is she won't
stay Milked.

—Anonymous

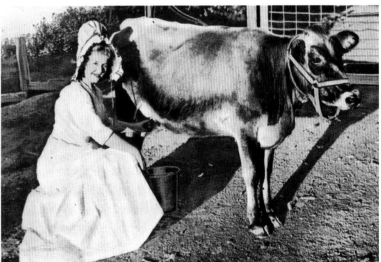

Milk the cow that standeth still.

—Proverb

AN47-003   AN47-002

AN47-004   AN47-008

AN47-005

AN47-006   AN47-007

AN47-001

> A **COW** is a very good animal in the field, but we turn her out of a garden.
>
> —Samuel Johnson

The browsing cows eyes open wide, as their mate the swaying figures glide.

AN48-003

AN48-002

AN48-004

AN48-008

AN48-007

AN48-005

AN48-006

AN48-001

Kiss till the cow comes home.

—Francis Beaumont

Union Stock Yards, Chicago.

Prize Cattle, Union Stock Yards, South Omaha, Neb.

An animal's eyes have the power to speak a great language.

—Martin Buber

AN49-003　　　　　　　　　　　　　　　　　AN49-002

AN49-004　　　　　　　　　　　　　　　　　AN49-008

AN49-005

AN49-006　　　　　　　　　　　　　　　　　AN49-007

That's a fine specimen of a **pig**.

—E. B. White *Charlotte's Web*

COUTUMES, MŒURS ET COSTUMES BRETONS
Départ pour le Marché (PLOUGASTEL).

AN50-003

AN50-002

AN50-004

AN50-007

AN50-005

AN50-006

50

AN50-001

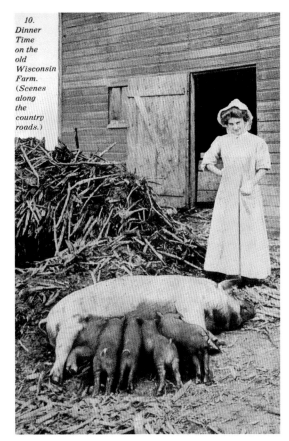

10. Dinner Time on the old Wisconsin Farm. (Scenes along the country roads.)

The End of the Route
Union Stock Yards
Chicago

A Lot of Suckers in Boston, Mass.

AN51-003   AN51-002

AN51-004

AN51-005   AN51-008

AN51-006   AN51-007

If you
can *walk*
you can
dance.
If you
can talk
you can
sing.

**—Zimbabwe
Proverb**

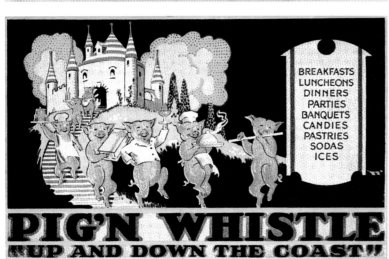

BREAKFASTS
LUNCHEONS
DINNERS
PARTIES
BANQUETS
CANDIES
PASTRIES
SODAS
ICES

PIG'N WHISTLE
"UP AND DOWN THE COAST"

AN52-004   AN52-003   AN52-002

                                                      AN52-007

AN52-005   AN52-006

"Sure and it would be the mighty proud pig, Miss Kathleen, if it knew you would be havin' yer breakfast off it some fine morning"

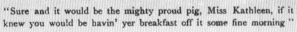

AN53-003   AN53-002

AN53-004   AN53-005

I
don't
think
anyone
has a
normal
family.

—Edward Furlong

TRY WRIGHT'S LITTLE LIVER PILLS.

AN54-003

AN54-002

AN54-004

AN54-005

AN54-007

AN54-006

You don't *love* someone because they're beautiful. They're beautiful because you *love* them.

—Anonymous

Oh, **Charley dear, did you come back to me.**

—Anonymous

AN55-003   AN55-002

AN55-004   AN55-007

AN55-005   AN55-006

God Jul

NEW YEAR GREETINGS

God Jul

A Happy New-Year.

AN56-003

AN56-002

AN56-004

AN56-005

AN56-008

AN56-006

AN56-007

AN56-001

THERE ARE 2 THINGS IN LIFE FOR WHICH WE ARE NEVER TRULY PREPARED:

TWINS.

—Josh Billings

FROGS have it easy, they can EAT what BUGS them.

—Unknown

AN57-003   AN57-002

AN57-004   AN57-008

AN57-005

AN57-006   AN57-007

AN57-001